For Andrew and Matthew Stimson
A.D.

The King of Kennelwick Castle
Text copyright © 1986 by Colin West
Illustrations copyright © 1986 by Anne Dalton
First published in Great Britain by Walker Books Ltd., London
Printed in Italy. All rights reserved.
Library of Congress Catalog Card Number: 85-46023
ISBN 0-694-00136-8
ISBN 0-397-32197-X
First American Edition

THE KING OF KENNELWICK CASTLE

by Colin West
pictures by Anne Dalton

J. B. Lippincott   New York

This is the King of Kennelwick Castle.

This is the boy
who carries a bundle
addressed to the King
of Kennelwick Castle.

To—
The King of
Kennelwick Castle

This is the mother
who serves the supper
to the boy called Barry
who carries a bundle
addressed to the King
of Kennelwick Castle.

This is the farmer
who churns the butter
to sell to the mother
who serves the supper
to the boy called Barry
who carries a bundle
addressed to the King
of Kennelwick Castle.

This is the milkmaid
who brings the fresh cream
to give to the farmer
who churns the butter
to sell to the mother
who serves the supper
to the boy called Barry
who carries a bundle
addressed to the King
of Kennelwick Castle.

This is the cow
in a meadow so green
who gives the milkmaid
her very best cream
to take to the farmer
who churns the butter
to sell to the mother
who serves the supper
to the boy called Barry
who carries a bundle
addressed to the King
of Kennelwick Castle.

This is the grass
that grows on the ground
where stands the cow
in a meadow so green
who gives the milkmaid
her very best cream
to take to the farmer
who churns the butter
to sell to the mother
who serves the supper
to the boy called Barry
who carries a bundle
addressed to the King
of Kennelwick Castle.

This is the rain
  that falls all around
    that waters the grass
      that grows on the ground
        where stands the cow
          in a meadow so green
            who gives the milkmaid
              her very best cream
                to take to the farmer
                  who churns the butter
                    to sell to the mother
                      who serves the supper
                        to the boy called Barry
                          who carries a bundle
                            addressed to the King
                              of Kennelwick Castle.

This is the King again,
in the rain,
the rain that seems
to fall all around
that waters the grass
that grows on the ground
where stands the cow
in a meadow so green
who gives the milkmaid
her very best cream
to take to the farmer
who churns the butter
to sell to the mother
who serves the supper
to the boy called Barry
who carries a bundle
addressed to the King
of Kennelwick Castle.

This is the present
from faraway Spain
that's being opened
by the King in the rain,
the rain that seems
to fall all around
that waters the grass
that grows on the ground
where stands the cow
in a meadow so green
who gives the milkmaid
her very best cream
to take to the farmer
who churns the butter
to sell to the mother
who serves the supper
to the boy called Barry
who carried the bundle
addressed to the King
of Kennelwick Castle.

And this is what
he found inside –
a green umbrella
tall and wide…

And look – the King's
no longer glum,
now that his birthday
present has come –
a present from
the Queen of Spain
to help the King
keep off the rain –
the rain that seems
to fall all around
that waters the grass
that grows on the ground
where stands the cow
in a meadow so green
who gives the milkmaid
her very best cream
to take to the farmer
who churns the butter
to sell to the mother
who serves the supper
to the boy called Barry
who carried the bundle
addressed to the King
of Kennelwick Castle.